D1150148

for Remy Charlip

Methuen/Moonlight
First published by Holiday House, New York
Text ©1977 by Steven Kroll
Illustrations ©1977 by Tomie de Paola
First published in Great Britain 1984 by Methuen
Children's Books Ltd, 11 New Fetter Lane, London EC4
in association with Moonlight Publishing Ltd
131 Kensington Church Street, London W8

Printed in Italy by La Editoriale Libraria

ISBN 0 907144 67 5

Santa's Crash-Bang Christmas

by Stephen Kroll
illustrated by Tomie de Paola

methuen ● moonlight

Santa landed his reindeer
on the Sylvesters' roof.
He fell out of his sleigh
and bumped his nose.

Santa sighed and shook his head.
Then he picked himself up
and searched in his pockets
for a handkerchief.

The handkerchief wasn't there,
and neither were the nose drops
for his sniffle.
He looked at his watch,
but it wasn't on his wrist.

"Oh dear," he said.
"Oh dear, oh dear.
It's going to be
one of those awful nights."

Then he tumbled down
the chimney into a pile of ashes.

Santa sat for a moment.

He brushed off his clothes,
stepped out of the fireplace,

and knocked over
the Christmas tree.

He stood perfectly still
in the middle of the living room.
"Oh no," he said.
"Not the Christmas tree."

Then he sat down on the sofa
and it collapsed.
"Oh dear," said Santa.
"Oh dear, oh dear."

He struggled off the sofa,
bumped into the chandelier,
and it fell on his head.
Santa rubbed his head.
"How I wish I was home,"
he sighed.

He opened his bag.
He'd brought a motorcycle
for Mum and Dad,
and a fish tank
and a toboggan for Jill.

Santa crawled inside his bag,
looking for more presents.
Then, *plop,* a polar bear
landed in his arms.

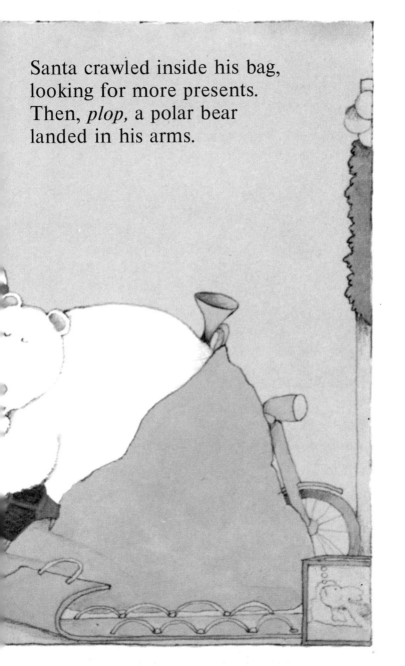

Santa stumbled back onto his feet
and bumped into Gerald, the elf.
"What are *you* doing here?"
asked Santa.
"Came for the ride," said Gerald.
"Thought it would be fun,
but it's not. It's too much work."

"Well, the job has to be done,"
said Santa.
"Now what am I going to do
with this polar bear?
It's in here by mistake."

"We'll take it along," said Gerald.
"Shouldn't we be going now?"

But just then, the polar bear
took off across the living room.

Santa hurried after it.

Then he thought
he heard the Sylvesters
moving around upstairs.
He hid in the hall cupboard.
The cupboard door fell off
  its hinges with a loud *boom*.

Santa left the cupboard,
knocked over the umbrella stand,
and heard the polar bear
running up the stairs.

Santa ran up after it,
tripped on the stairs,
knocked a picture off the wall,

stumbled onto the landing,
blundered into
Mum and Dad's room,
and saw the polar bear
vanish out of the window.

"Merry Christmas,"
Santa whispered,
as he tiptoed by the bed.

"Happy New Year,"
Santa said, as he teetered
on the window ledge.

In a moment,
he was struggling to the roof.

In another moment,
he had caught the polar bear
and stuffed it in the sleigh.

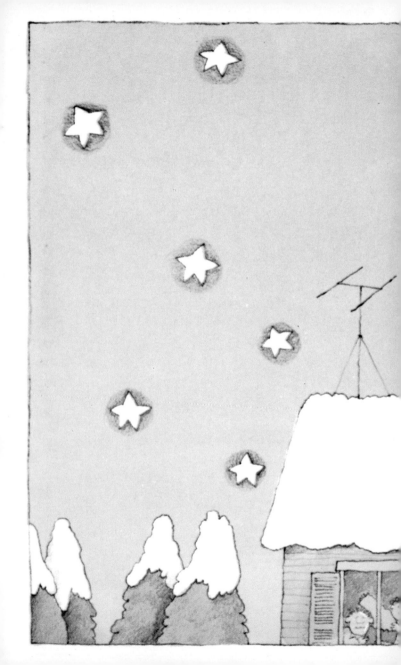

As he flew off into the night,
Mum and Dad and Jill woke up,
pulled on their dressing gowns,

and dashed
down the stairs...

to see their presents.

Mr Potter's Pigeon by Reg Cartwright
The moving story of an old man and his pet racing pigeon; award-winning pictures.

King Nonn the Wiser by Colin McNaughton
The hilarious adventures of a brave but short-sighted knight.

The Pigs' Wedding by Helme Heine
A day full of surprises, fun and happiness for Trotter and Curlytail.

The Friends' Racing Cart by Helme Heine
Johnny Mouse's friends are quick to the rescue when his fast cart goes out of control.

Hare and Badger Go to Town by Naomi Lewis and Tony Ross
The modern fable of how Hare and Badger fare with city life.

Jack and the Beanstalk by Tony Ross
One of Tony Ross' best-known revivals of traditional fairy tales.

The Greedy Little Cobbler by Tony Ross
Why the little cobbler is the worst shod of all.

The Little Moon Theatre by Irene Haas
The troop of travelling players makes wishes come true...

The Hairy Monster by Henriette Bichonnier and Pef
Little Princess Lucy is cheeky but far cleverer than the horrible Hairy Monster who wants to gobble her up.

Panda's Puzzle by Michael Foreman
Panda travels from the Himalayas to the United States to find the answer to a very important question.

Lola at the Riverbank and
Lola and the Dandelion Mystery by Yvan Pommaux
In these two enchanting books, Lola the little vole asks her father questions about nature that intrigue all children.

See You in the Morning! and
The Higher and Higher House by Janosch
Each title contains several short tales about Snoddle and his friends, full of comical details, riddles and games.